Your Head's not the Place to store Problems in

For Sarah-Quynh, problem sharer since 2004 xx. J.P.

For Josh whose lyrical ways found a space in The Magic Bus (family + dogs + Josh). Happy days! S.M.K.

Scholastic Press
An imprint of Scholastic Australia Pty Limited
PO Box 579 Gosford NSW 2250
ABN 11 000 614 577
www.scholastic.com.au

Part of the Scholastic Group
Sydney · Auckland · New York · Toronto · London · Mexico City
New Delhi · Hong Kong · Buenos Aires · Puerto Rico

Published by Scholastic Australia in 2023.

NATIONAL LIBRARY OF AUSTRALIA

A catalogue record for this book is available from the National Library of Australia

ISBN: 978-1-76129-302-3

Stephen Michael King created these illustrations digitally.
Typeset in Macarons.

Printed in China by RR Donnelley.
Scholastic Australia's policy, in association with RR Donnelley, is to use papers that are renewable and made efficiently from wood grown in responsibly managed forests, so as to minimise its environmental footprint.

10 9 8 7 6 5 4 3 25 26 27 28 29 / 2

Your head's not the place to store problems in

Josh Pyke

Stephen Michael King

A Scholastic Press book from Scholastic Australia

I have a friend

with a normal-sized mind

(though the size of a mind is quite hard to define).

This normal-sized mind
can bear quite a load,
but sometimes this mind feels like it might **explode**.

The problems seem **heavy,**

they **weigh**

my friend

down,

their mind
is all
CLUTTERED,
the world seems too **LOUd!**

We're full to the brim
with unknowable things

but your mind's not the place to store problems in.

I have a friend
with a normal-sized brain
that at times seems too small
for the thoughts it contains.

Some thoughts are enormous

and others

quite small,

but my friend has this brain that cannot fit them all.

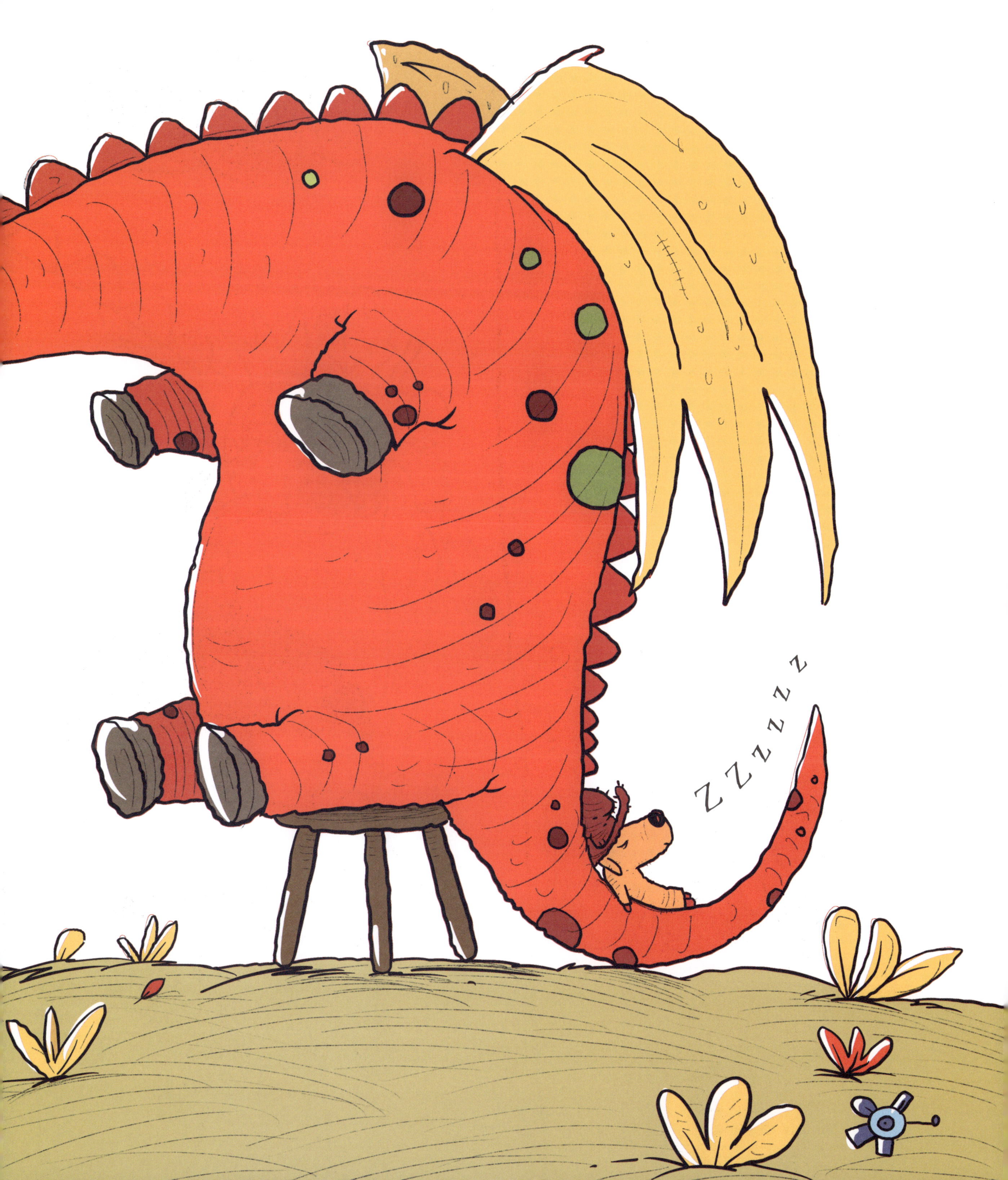
ZZzzzz

Sometimes my friend's brain feels **full up**

and **crowdy**

and their **mood**

swings from

sunny

to **suddenly**

cloudy.

We're full to the brim with unknowable things

and your brain's not the place to store problems in.

I have a friend with a normal-sized life
who at times feels it's bulging
with trouble and strife.

And things seem much worse
than they probably are
in the scheme of the normal-sized life lived
so far.

And the trouble e x p a n d s,

the strife seems to double.

Will this normal-sized life simply burst like a bubble?

We're full to the brim

with unknowable things,

so your life's not the place

to store problems in.

So where then to store all these stresses and strife?

The questions and problems that come with a life
and lodge in the brain and get stuck in the mind?
Where is the place for these troubles we find?

Well, you see,

here's the thing,

here's the rub,

here's the key!

They shouldn't be stored.

They

should

be set free!

You

simply

MUST

share

them.

YES! Say them out loud!

Don't bottle them up.

NO! LET THEM ALL OUT!

Because once they're shared and let out,
then you'll find,

that there's space to fit

much kinder thoughts

in your mind.

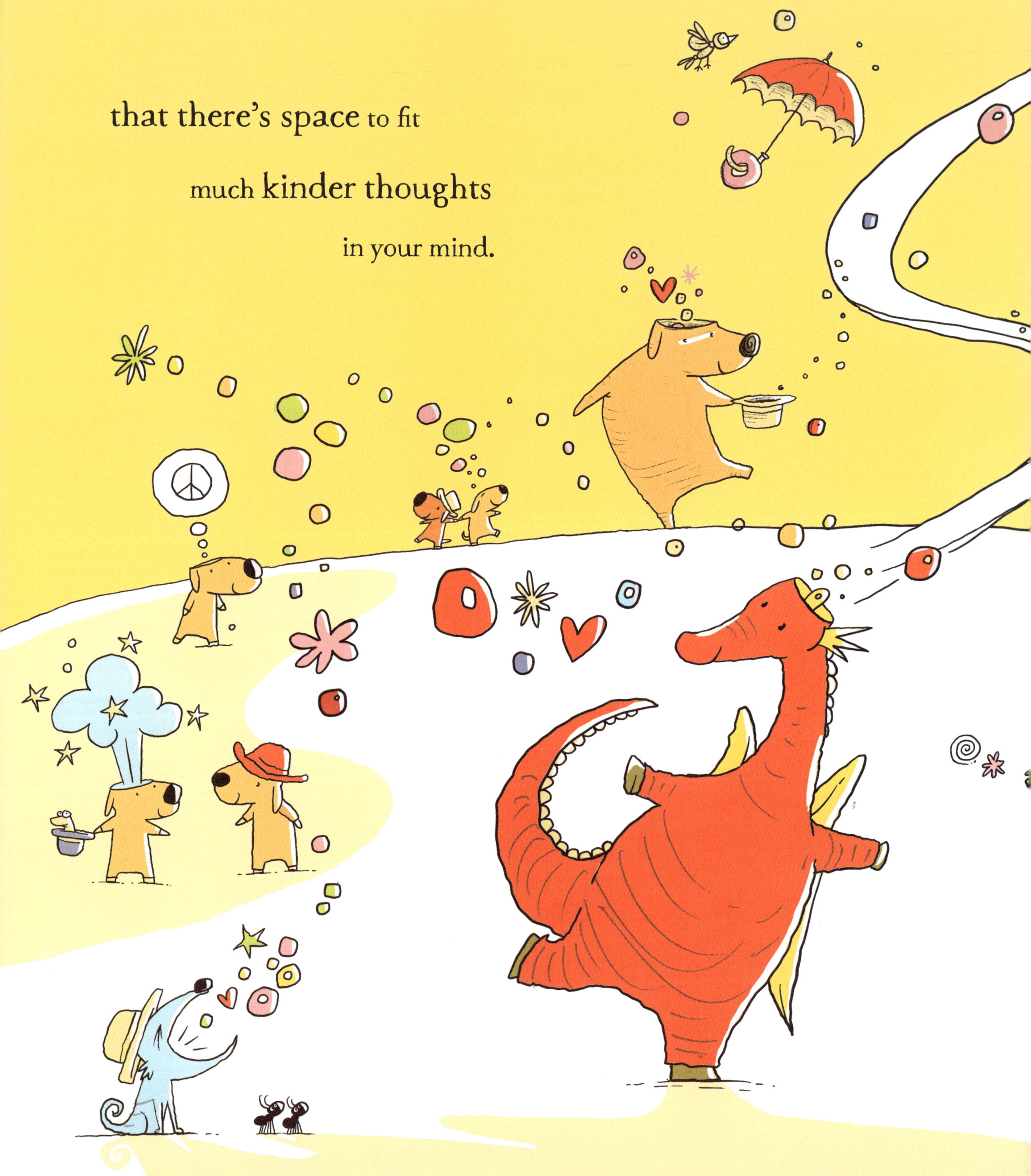

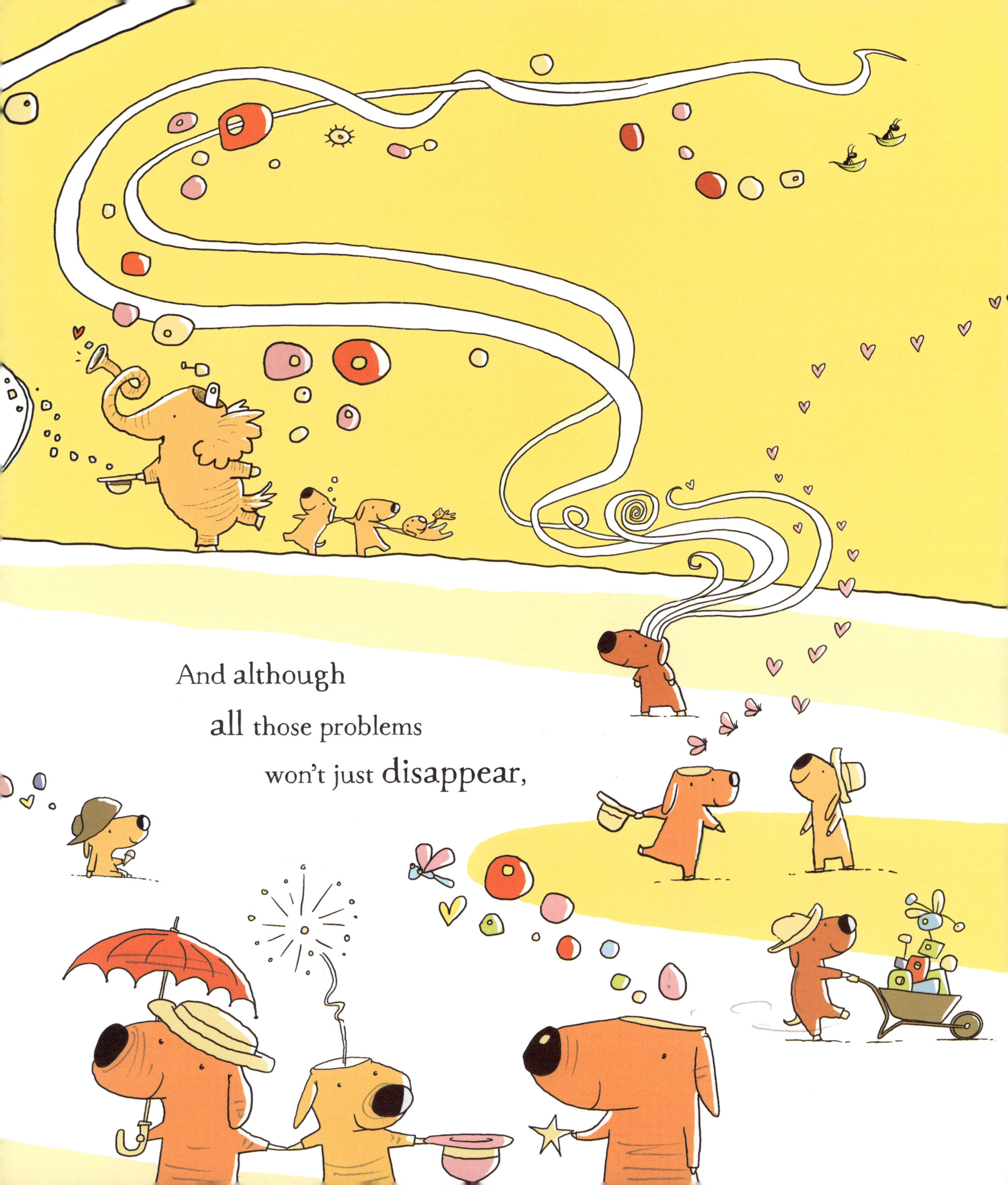

And although
all those problems
won't just disappear,

they'll become
things to learn from,
not simply
to fear.

We're full to the brim

with unknowable things,

but your head's not the place

to store

problems

in.

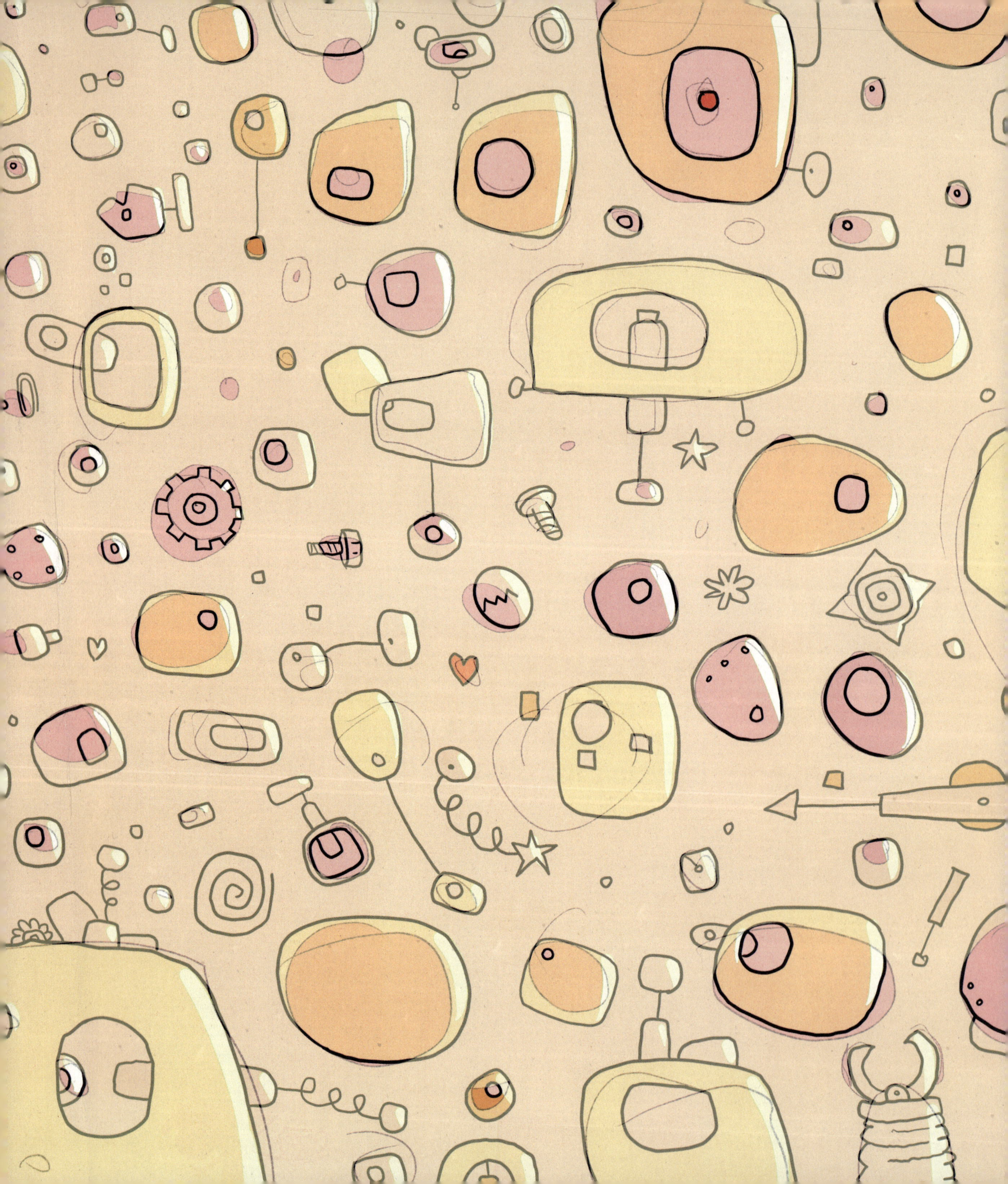